THE FUNNY DREAM

KAETHE ZEMACH-BERSIN

GREENWILLOW BOOKS

NEW YORK

Thanks to Uri Orlev

Watercolor paints were used for the full-color art.
The text type is ITC Caslon No. 224 Medium.

Copyright © 1988 by Kaethe Zemach-Bersin
All rights reserved. No part of this book
may be reproduced or utilized in any form
or by any means, electronic or mechanical,
including photocopying, recording or by
any information storage and retrieval
system, without permission in writing
from the Publisher, Greenwillow Books,
a division of William Morrow & Company, Inc.,
105 Madison Avenue, New York, N.Y. 10016.
Printed in Hong Kong by South China Printing Co.
First Edition
10 9 8 7 6 5 4 3 2 1

Library of Congress Cataloging-in-Publication Data

Zemach-Bersin, Kaethe.
The funny dream/by Kaethe Zemach-Bersin.
p.   cm.
Summary: A child has a dream in which
she grows big, her parents become small,
and she must get them ready for school.
ISBN 0-688-07500-2.   ISBN 0-688-07501-0 (lib. bdg.)
[1. Dreams—Fiction.   2. Parent and child—Fiction.]
I. Title   PZ7.Z416Fu   1988
[E]—dc 19   87-18769   CIP   AC

For David, Ariella,
Cybele, and Talya,

with love

One night while I was sleeping in my bed, I had a funny dream.

I dreamed that it was morning,

and I got out of bed feeling

very big and strong.

I went into my parents' room to say good morning,
and they were so surprised to see me!

"Oh my," they said, "you are all grown up!"

"That's right," I said, "and now you are smaller than I am!"

"Come on, little Mommy, let's go, little Daddy,
it's time to get dressed. It's time to eat breakfast,
and it's time to get ready for school."

My mother didn't want me to wash her face,

and my father didn't want to get dressed.

"You can't catch me," he said,

and he ran away.

I chased my little daddy

all over the house—

until I caught him.

When I brushed my mother's hair, there were
lots of tangles. Then she wanted ribbons—
blue ribbons—but we only had pink ones.

They spilled their juice on the floor,

and when breakfast was over

the kitchen was a mess.

My father said he wanted more butter
and a different kind of cereal. My mother
said she didn't like scrambled eggs.

Next came breakfast. My mother sat on a telephone book

and my father sat in the high chair.

I gave them both toast and cereal, scrambled eggs,

and orange juice.

Then my father tripped over a toy and
bumped his nose on the edge of a chair.

I gave him one Band-Aid and three kisses.

I had some trouble finding my father's and
mother's shoes. One shoe was under the couch,
and another was hiding in the doll's house.

I gave my little mother a piggy-back ride,

and I gave my little father a piggy-back ride.

At last my mother and father

went off to school.

"Bye-bye," I called.

"Have a nice time.

I'll see you later!"

The rest of the day was boring. The house was very quiet, and there wasn't much to do. I didn't feel like cleaning up the kitchen, or washing the dishes, or picking up the toys.

No one was around to read to me

or take me anywhere.

And worse than that, I missed my friends.

So when my dream ended,
I was glad to wake up and
have a regular day.

When I got to school, I told my friends about my funny dream, and we hung on the climbing bars and laughed and laughed and laughed.